GOING HOME

By Eve Bunting

Illustrated by David Diaz

Joanna Cotler Books * HarperCollinsPublishers

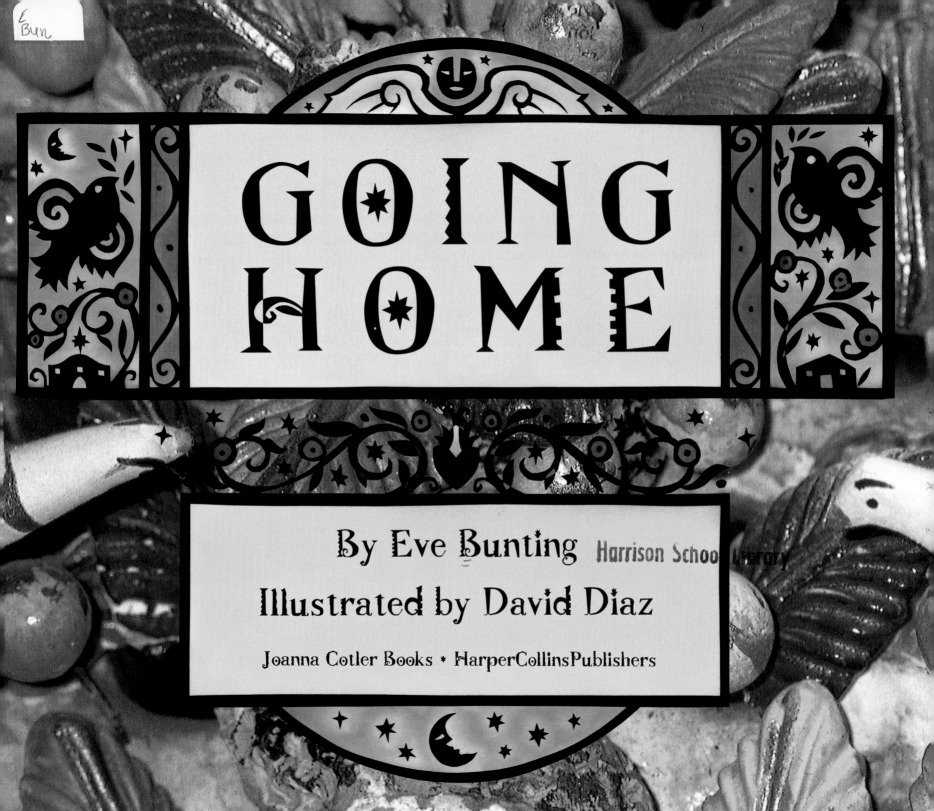

Library of Congress Cataloging-in-Publication Data

Bunting, Eve, date

Going home / by Eve Bunting ; illustrated by David Diaz.

p.   cm.

"Joanna Cotler books."

Summary: Although a Mexican family comes to the United States to work as farm laborers
so that their children will have opportunities, the parents still consider Mexico their home.

ISBN 0-06-026296-6. — ISBN 0-06-026297-4 (lib. bdg.)

1. Mexicans—United States—Juvenile fiction [1. Mexicans—
United States—Fiction. 2. Migrant labor—Fiction. 3. Home—Fiction.]

I. Diaz, David, ill.   II. Title.

PZ7.B9152Go 1996 95-35323

[E]—dc20 CIP

AC

1 2 3 4 5 6 7 8 9 10
❖
First Edition

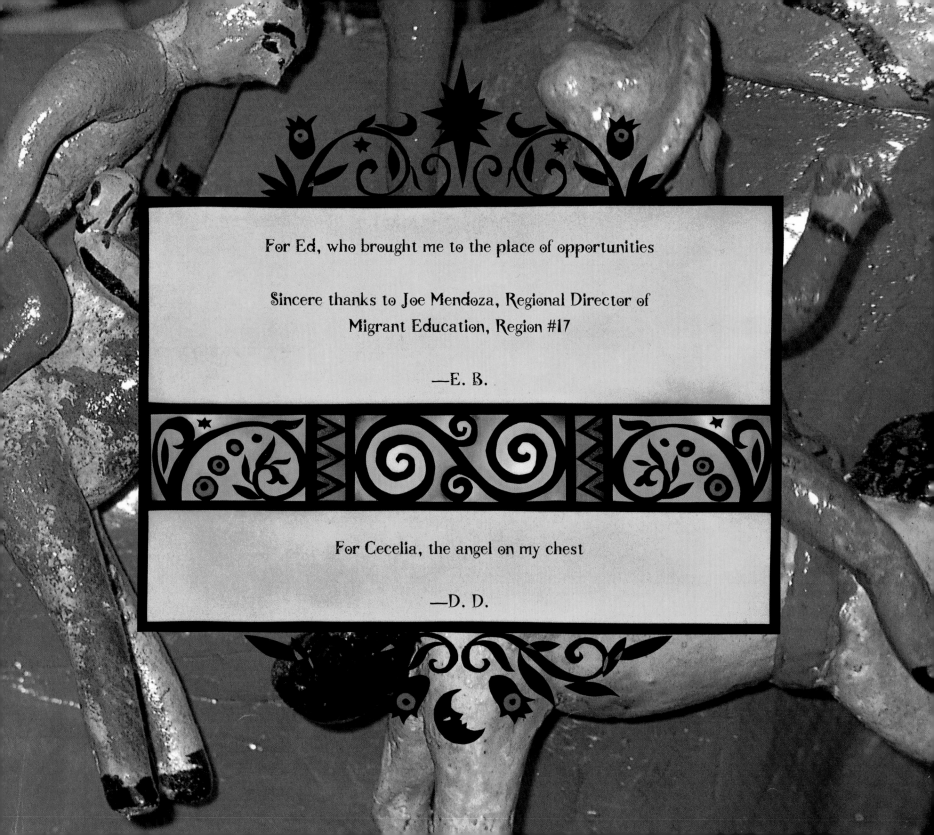

For Ed, who brought me to the place of opportunities

Sincere thanks to Joe Mendoza, Regional Director of
Migrant Education, Region #17

—E. B.

For Cecelia, the angel on my chest

—D. D.

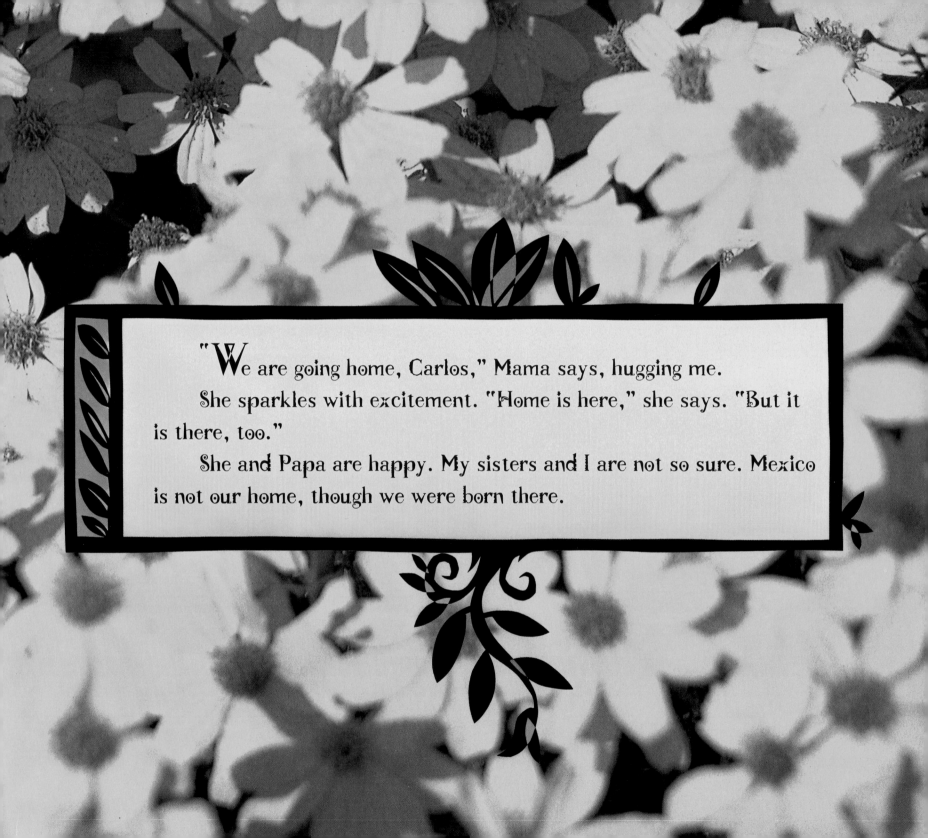

"We are going home, Carlos," Mama says, hugging me.

She sparkles with excitement. "Home is here," she says. "But it is there, too."

She and Papa are happy. My sisters and I are not so sure. Mexico is not our home, though we were born there.

Papa piles our boxes and suitcases into the back of our old station wagon. He slides in our battered cooler, which is filled with food and cold drinks for the journey. My little sister, Nora, and my big sister, Dolores, get into the back seat with me. Nora is five, Dolores is ten.

Papa locks the door of our house. The house really belongs to Mr. Culloden, the labor manager, but it is ours as long as we work the crops for him. It has been ours for almost five years.

Almost everyone in our camp has come out to see us off.

Nora waves to her best friend, Maria.

"Don't be sad, *Norita*," Dolores says. "We are only going for Christmas. You will see Maria again soon."

We're on our way!

It is a long drive to our parents' village of La Perla, and we are a little nervous as we cross the border into Mexico.

"Are you sure they will let us back, Papa?" I ask.

"Of course. Do not worry. We are legal farm workers. We have our *papeles*."

"Papers, Papa," I say quickly.

"Sí. Papeles." Papa speaks always in Spanish. He and Mama have no English. There is no need for it in the fields. But I'm always trying to teach them.

Now we are in Mexico.

I see no difference, but Mama does.

"Mexico! Mexico!" She blows kisses at the sun-filled winter sky.

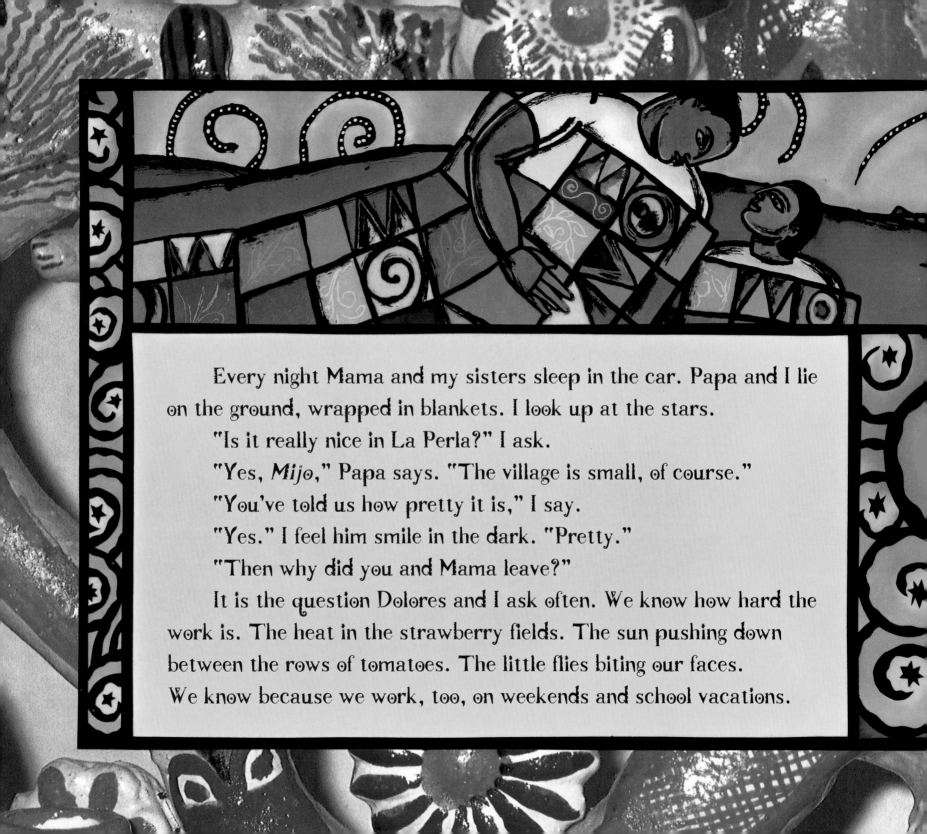

Every night Mama and my sisters sleep in the car. Papa and I lie on the ground, wrapped in blankets. I look up at the stars.

"Is it really nice in La Perla?" I ask.

"Yes, *Mijo*," Papa says. "The village is small, of course."

"You've told us how pretty it is," I say.

"Yes." I feel him smile in the dark. "Pretty."

"Then why did you and Mama leave?"

It is the question Dolores and I ask often. We know how hard the work is. The heat in the strawberry fields. The sun pushing down between the rows of tomatoes. The little flies biting our faces. We know because we work, too, on weekends and school vacations.

We see how tired Mama and Papa are at night. How Papa rubs Mama's shoulders. How stiffly he moves. "Why did you ever leave?" we ask.

"There is no work in La Perla. We are here for the opportunities." It is always the same answer.

Sometimes, behind his back, Dolores imitates Papa. "'We are here for the opportunities.' I don't see them getting many of these wonderful opportunities." Dolores is very grown-up and cool. That is why Mama worries about her.

Now I lie in Mexico, close to Papa, and watch a shooting star speed across the sky. I make a wish.

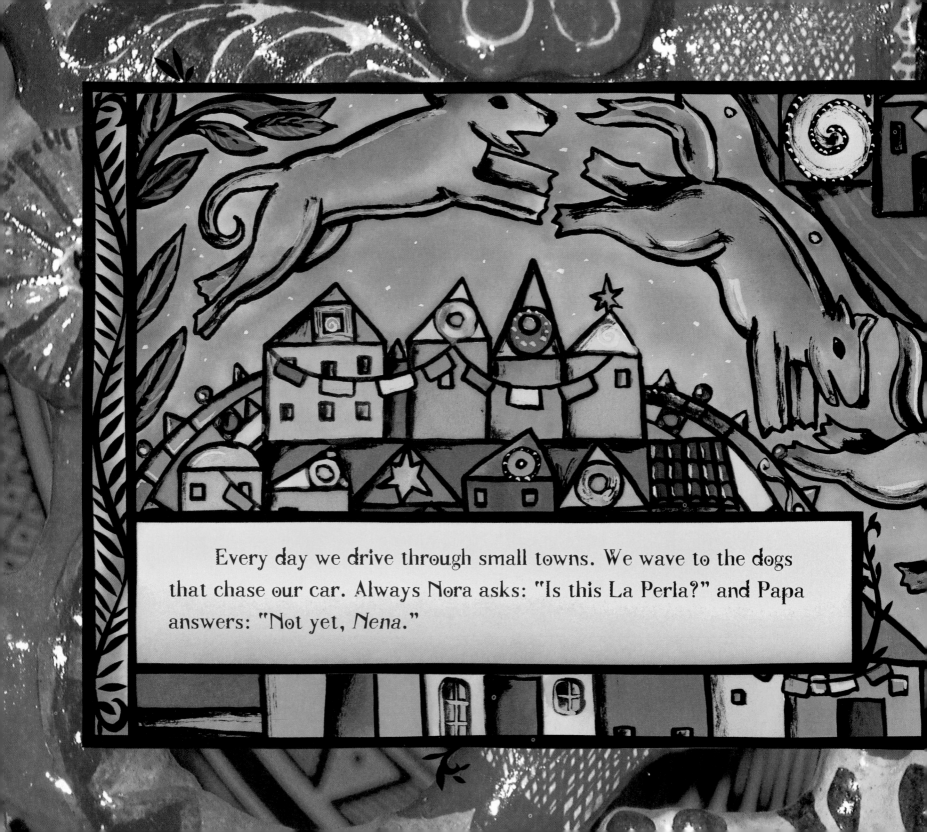

Every day we drive through small towns. We wave to the dogs that chase our car. Always Nora asks: "Is this La Perla?" and Papa answers: "Not yet, *Nena*."

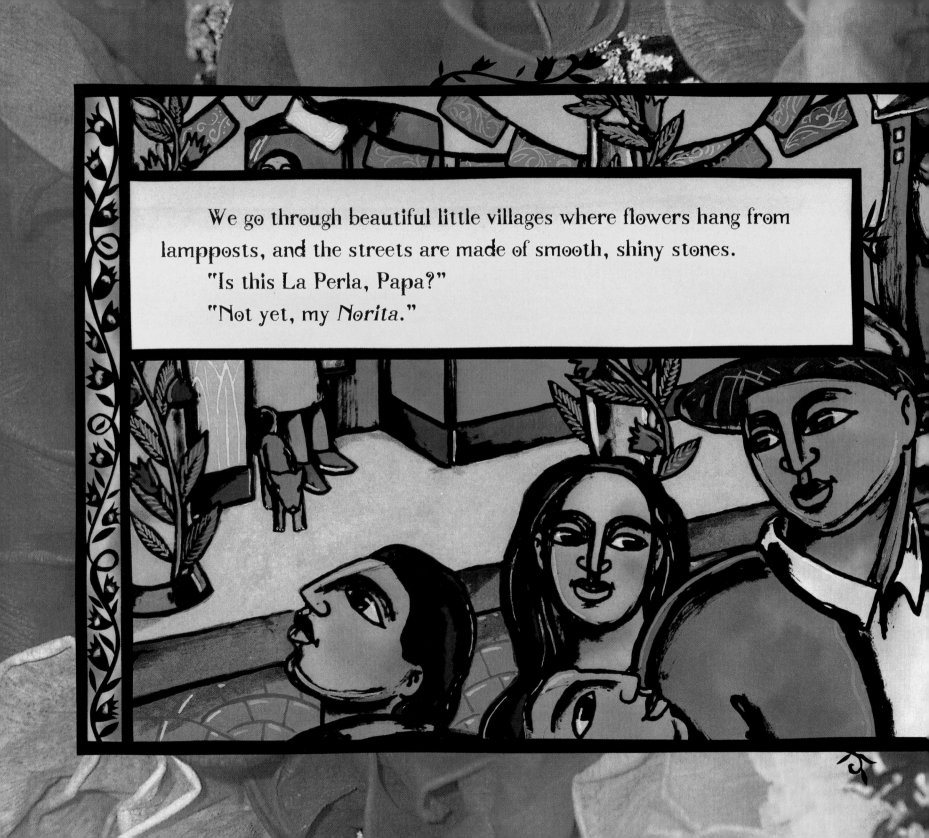

We go through beautiful little villages where flowers hang from lampposts, and the streets are made of smooth, shiny stones.

"Is this La Perla, Papa?"

"Not yet, my *Norita*."

We meet buses.

We pass men and women on bicycles.

We see an old man leading a burro that is piled high with firewood. He stops to stare.

Sometimes we have to go slowly because there are sheep on the road, sheep thick with their winter wool.

On the fourth evening we come to La Perla. Nora has stopped asking, and we don't know till Mama tells us.

Our car bumps along the street, which is decorated for Christmas with paper cutouts strung together—red and pink and yellow and blue. There is a scattering of houses, a general store, a big water tank, a church with a tinsel star on top. It is like a lot of the villages we have come through.

Papa honks the horn, and that brings people to their doors. He rolls down his window. "It is José and Consuelo and their family, home for Christmas," he shouts.

"José! Consuelo!"

"Beautiful children," they say. "Such nice clothes they have, Consuelo."

Mama smiles. "They're not their best."

Children crowd around us, and then I hear Mama say in a choked voice: "There is your Grandfather! And Aunt Ana!"

An old man comes out of one of the houses and behind him a tall, skinny woman with wide black hair.

"She looks like an umbrella," Dolores whispers, and giggles. Nora is making herself small and sucking her thumb. Nora is very shy.

There is a wooden plow outside Grandfather's house. I remember when Mama and Papa saved the money for it. Later they also sent money for two oxen. I wonder where the oxen are and if we will be friends.

Grandfather and Aunt Ana hug us. They don't feel like strangers.

That night, everyone in La Perla comes to Grandfather's house. The walls bulge with talk and rememberings. I have never seen Mama and Papa so lively.

"Say something in English," a woman asks me, and everyone is quiet, waiting.

I don't know what to say. "It is good to be here," I stammer at last.

They laugh and clap. "Imagine, Consuelo! Your son—and all your children—speaking English. So smart!"

"Yes," Papa says. "Their school is very fine. They are getting a good education."

The woman nods. "You were wise to take them and go. Our school is good, too. But where are the opportunities for our children after?"

I blink. There is that word again.

"We were wise," Mama says. "But it was hard. It is still hard." She sounds so sad that it scares me. But soon she is laughing again.

I am beginning to understand something.

It is late when everyone leaves. Mama and Papa sleep on the floor in Grandfather's house, and we sleep in the car. It is not dark, because there is a Christmas-coming moon, and a few of the houses still have friendly lights in their windows.

"You will be all right," Mama says cheerfully. "It is safe here."

Nora lies between Dolores and me. We wait to talk till she is asleep.

"Mama and Papa like it here a lot," I whisper.

Something big pokes its face against the car window, and I jump. But it is only a curious cow that somehow got free.

"La Perla is pretty," I say. "But I thought it would be more special. I thought that was why they like it."

"I don't think that's why," Dolores begins, and I wait for more, because Dolores knows a lot. But instead she says, "Sh! Be asleep!"

Someone is coming out of Grandfather's house. It is Mama in her new white nightgown, and Papa in his striped pajamas.

I half-close my eyes.

Mama opens the car door and pulls our blanket higher on us. *"Angelitos,"* she murmurs.

And then . . . then, it's so weird. She and Papa start to dance. There is no music, but they dance barefoot in the street. Dogs unwind themselves to come sniff at their legs. My curious cow watches with interest. Mama and Papa ignore them.

Dolores and I stretch our necks to watch.

"Mama looks so young and beautiful," Dolores whispers. "And Papa . . . so handsome."

"She has forgotten about her sore shoulders," I say.

"And he's forgotten about his bad knees," Dolores adds.

They dance and dance. Papa's cheek is against Mama's hair. I see that he is whispering to her. I feel as if I shouldn't be watching, and I lie down again. Dolores does, too.

After a while we hear Grandfather's door close, and we can tell they've gone inside.

There is a terrible ache in my chest. They love it here because it's home. They left home for us.

"Carlos?" Dolores says. "Do you know Mama and Papa are saving money? They plan to come back someday and live in Grandfather's house and work his land."

"For sure?" I ask.

"For sure," Dolores says. "I listen when they talk."

That makes me smile. I know Dolores listens. That's why she knows so much.

"Good," I say, and I think, It will be after our opportunities.

I picture them back here, dancing in the streets of La Perla, and I lie there, watching the moon shine on the Christmas star till I fall asleep.

Let's Explore

How many are there?

by Henry Pluckrose

SEA-TO-SEA

Mankato Collingwood London

Author's note

This book is one of a series which has been designed to encourage young readers to think about the everyday concepts that form part of their world. The text and photographs complement each other, and both elements combine to provide starting points for discussion. Although each book is complete in itself, each title links closely with others in the set, so presenting an ideal platform for learning.

I have consciously avoided "writing down" to my readers. Young children like to know the "real" words for things, and are better able to express themselves when they can use correct terms with confidence.

Young children learn from the experiences they share with adults around them. The child offers his or her ideas, which are then developed and extended through the adult. The books in this series are a means for the child and adult to share informal talk, photographs, and text, and the ideas, which accompany them.

One particular element merits comment. Information books are also reading books. Like a successful storybook, an effective information book will be turned to again and again. As children develop, their appreciation of the significance of fact develops too. The young child who asks "What is a number?" may subsequently and more provocatively ask, "What is the biggest number in the world?" Thoughts take time to generate. Hopefully books like those in this series provide the momentum for this.

Henry Pluckrose

Contents

One, two, three, four, five...
Everywhere you look,
you can see numbers.
On the door of your house,
on the front of the bus,
on your telephone.
Where else can you
see numbers?

Each number has a different shape.
Numbers can be written
in figures and in words.

Can you match these words
to the figures opposite?

one   two   three   four

five   six   seven

eight   nine   ten

There are lots of sheep
on the hillside.

We use numbers to count the sheep.
How many sheep can you count?

When you were small,
you probably used your hands
to help you to count to ten.

11

How many oranges are there?

Danielle adds two more oranges.
How many oranges
are there now?

How many children are at the party?
Two of the children go home.

Take away two children.
How many children are left?

How many pieces of cake
can you count?
Divide the cake
between the children.
How many pieces
will each child have?

How many trucks are there?
Do you know how many wheels
are on each truck?
Two sets of four wheels
equals eight wheels in all.

20

Sometimes we count in groups.
We have special words
for groups of numbers.
A "pair" is a group of two.
What kinds of things
come in pairs?

How many shoes are there?
How many pairs can you make?

We call six an "even" number.
It can be divided into pairs.

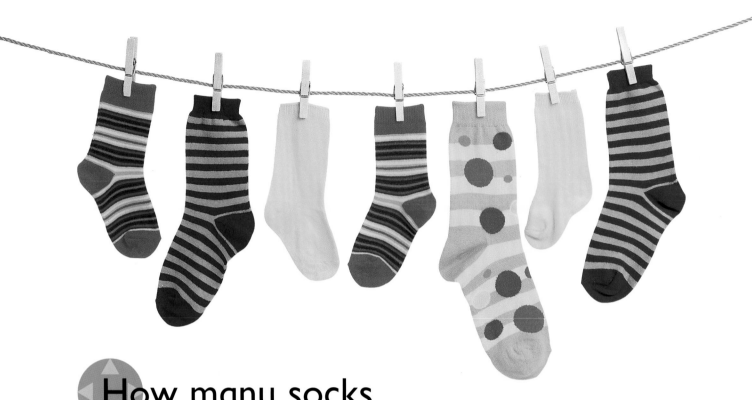

How many socks
are hanging
on this laundry line?

24

How many pairs can you make?

Seven is an "odd" number.
When we put the socks into pairs,
there is one sock left over.

The children are running a race. Jack is the winner, because he came first. Ben came second. Josh came third.

Who will stand on block one?
Who will stand on blocks
two and three?

We can use numbers to measure.

We can measure weight.

We can measure size.

We can measure distance.

How many miles
away is Paris?

It is easier to count small numbers,
but sometimes we need
to count large numbers too.
You could even count
all the people in this crowd!

100—one hundred

1,000—one thousand

1,000,000—one million

Index

This edition first published in 2007 by
Sea-to-Sea Publications
1980 Lookout Drive
North Mankato
Minnesota 56003

Copyright © Sea-to-Sea Publications 2007

Printed in China

Library of Congress Cataloging-in-Publication Data:

Pluckrose, Henry Arthur
    How many are there? / by Henry Pluckrose
    p. cm. -- (Let's explore, math set)
    Includes index.
    ISBN-13: 978-1-59771-037-4
    1. Arithmetic--Juvenile literature. 2.
Counting--Juvenile literature. 3. Numeration--
Juvenile literature. I. Title.

QA115.P624 2006
513--dc22
                                2005056756

9 8 7 6 5 4 3 2

Published by arrangement with the Watts
Publishing Group Ltd, London

Series editor: Louise John
Series designer: Jason Anscomb
Series consultant: Peter Patilla
Picture Credits:
Steve Shott Photography pp. cover and title page, 6, 11, 12,
13, 14, 15, 16, 19, 20, 22, 23, 24, 25, 27; Bubbles pp. 26 (Jennie
Woodcock); The Stock Market p. 29; AA Photo Library
p. 28; Bruce Coleman p. 8/9 (Jorg & Petra Wegner); Robert
Harding p. 31; Image Bank p. 4 (Grant Faint).
With thanks to our models: Reid Burns, Karim Chehab,
Alex Dymock, Melissa Eedle, Danielle Grimmett-Gardiner,
Charlie Newton, Robert Orbeney, Alice Snedden.